For Nikolai
—C.B.

For little Zoey Zoo,
who was along for the whole ride
—R.K.

CLARION BOOKS

3 Park Avenue, New York, New York 10016

Text copyright © 2017 by Carol Brendler • Illustrations copyright © 2017 by Renée Kurilla

All rights reserved. For information about permission to reproduce selections from this book, write to
trade.permissions@hmhco.com or to Permissions, Houghton Mifflin Harcourt Publishing Company, 3 Park Avenue,
19th Floor, New York, New York 10016. • Clarion Books is an imprint of Houghton Mifflin Harcourt Publishing Company.
www.hmhco.com • The text was set in Humper and Mrs. Lollipop. • Book design by Sharismar Rodriguez

Library of Congress Cataloging-in-Publication Data is available. • ISBN 978-0-544-83958-8

Manufactured in China • SCP 10 9 8 7 6 5 4 3 2 1 • 4500654529

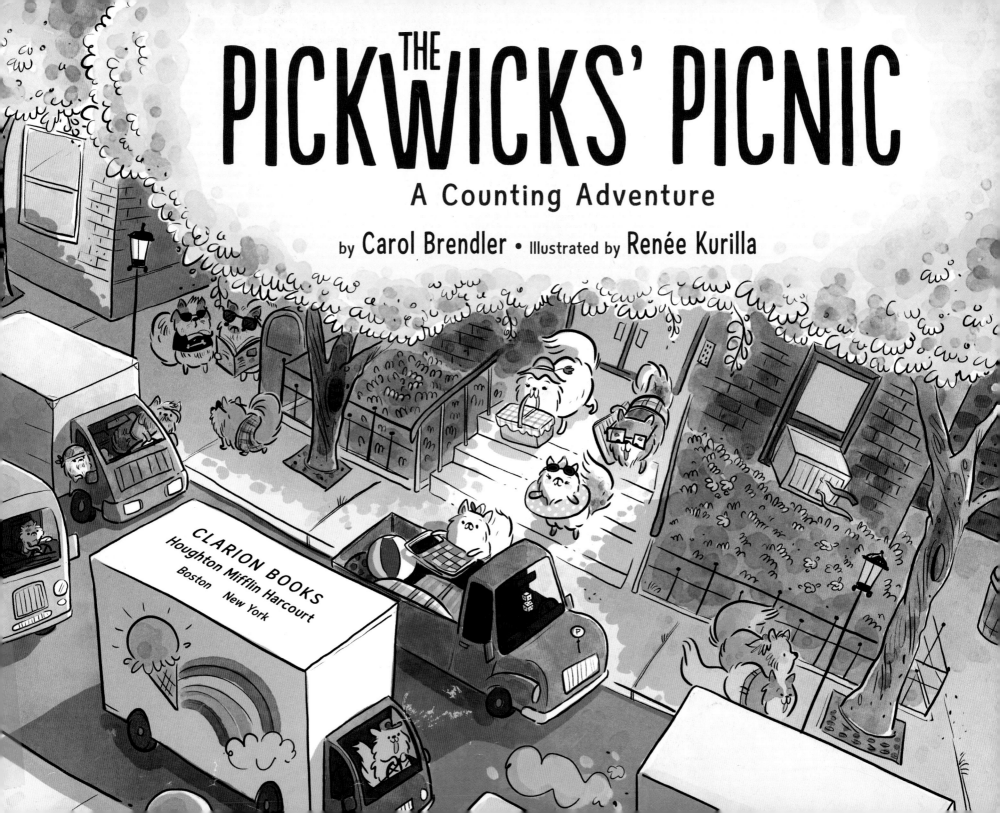

THE PICKWICKS' PICNIC

A Counting Adventure

by **Carol Brendler** • Illustrated by **Renée Kurilla**

CLARION BOOKS
Houghton Mifflin Harcourt
Boston   New York

It's hot. It's crowded. Traffic is a mighty, mighty mess. So Mom and Daddy, Pip and Peach, load up their trusty Pickwick pickup.

"Tally-ho!" says Pip.

"Off we go!" says Peach.

They're heading for the shore!

Goodbye, noise and heat and haze.

The Pickwicks in their pickup
leave the city far behind.

"Traffic's cleared!" says Pip.
"Disappeared!" says Peach.

Just **1** pickup, heading for the box-girder bridge, until—

2 blue scooters rumble
past the Pickwick pickup,
heading for the box-girder bridge;

3
squeaky jeeps overtake
the Pickwick pickup, heading
for the box-girder bridge;

4 family vans chug by the Pickwick pickup,
heading for the box-girder bridge;

5 flashy bikes come around the Pickwick pickup,
heading for the box-girder bridge;

6 ritzy limos whiz by
the Pickwick pickup,
heading for the box-girder bridge;

7 revvin' racers pass up the Pickwick pickup,
heading for the box-girder bridge;

8 hasty hatchbacks zing by the Pickwick pickup,

heading for the box-girder bridge;

9 hydraulic haulers breeze by the Pickwick pickup, heading for the box-girder bridge, and then—

10 troopers' cruisers block . . .

9 hydraulic haulers, **8** hasty hatchbacks, **7** revvin' racers, **6** ritzy limos, **5** flashy bikes, **4** family vans, **3** squeaky jeeps, and **2** blue scooters,

and they block the Pickwick pickup so that . . .

. . . *nobody* can go across the box-girder bridge!

"Uh-oh," says Pip.

"Oh, no," says Peach.

It's a mighty, mighty mess.

Bikers seethe; truckers smolder. They're idling in neutral at the box-girder bridge.

In a crush of noise and heat and haze, they wait and wait and wait and wait.

But Pip and Peach aren't fazed.

Peach unfolds a chair, Pip pours lemonade,
and Pip and Peach put up an awning,
making unexpected shade.

It's an unplanned Pickwick picnic
by the box-girder bridge!

Evening comes, lights go on, and look—
the barricades are gone!

The pickup's loaded up to cross the bridge, and go beyond.

Engines growl back to life.

10 cruisers, **9** haulers, **8** hatchbacks, **7** racers, **6** limos, **5** bikes,

4 vans, 3 jeeps, and 2 scooters board the bridge to parts unknown . . .

. . . and the Pickwick family glides across the box-girder bridge to the beachfront just ahead.

No noise, no heat, no haze . . . no traffic anymore.
Just *one* trusty Pickwick pickup and the Pickwicks, at the shore.